Clifford THE BIG RED DOG®

THE SNOW CHAMPION

by Carol Pugiano-Martin
Illustrated by Steve Haefele

Based on the Scholastic book series
"Clifford The Big Red Dog"
by Norman Bridwell

Designed by Michael Massen

ISBN 0-439-80845-6

12 11 10 9 8 7 6 5 4 3 6 7 8 9 10/0

Printed in the U.S.A.
First printing, January 2006

It was morning on Birdwell Island.

Everything was covered with snow.

So was Clifford!

"Look, Clifford! It snowed!" shouted

Emily Elizabeth.

She ran to put on her snow clothes.

T-Bone came into the yard.

“Look, Clifford, it snowed,” he said.

T-Bone looked sad.

“Hey, T,” said Clifford. “Why are you sad about the snow?”

Cleo ran into the yard.

Her tail wagged happily.

"Snowball fight! Snowball fight!" she shouted.

"That's why I'm sad," said T-Bone.

He seemed even sadder as he looked down at the snow.

“Are you afraid of the yearly snowball fight?”

asked Clifford.

“I sure am,” said T-Bone. “I don’t like getting hit with snowballs.”

"You don't have to be afraid, T-Bone," said Clifford.

"The snowball fight is friendly and fun. And we'll all be together."

"Besides," said Cleo, "those little old snowballs don't really hurt."

"That's easy for you to say, Cleo," said T-Bone. "You're a really fast runner."

"Here's the best part," said Cleo. "This year we will build forts. The forts will have flags on top. We'll play capture the flag and have a snowball fight at the same time!"

"I don't get it," said T-Bone nervously.

"That's okay. The kids will explain when we get there," said Clifford.

Clifford, T-Bone, and Cleo met Emily Elizabeth and Charley at the park. Both teams worked very hard on their forts.

Finally, the teams put their flags on their forts.

The forts looked great!

Jetta explained the rules.

"Okay, everyone. Each team will try to take the other team's flag. But if you get hit with a snowball, you have to go back to your fort and start over."

Everyone listened to Jetta except for T-Bone.

He was hiding behind his team's fort!

“If you win,” said Jetta, “you get to do whatever you want for a whole day. If I win, and I probably will, I will be Queen for a Day. Mac will be a prince.”

"What will you do if you win, Emily Elizabeth?" asked Charley.

"Oh, it doesn't matter, Charley," said Emily Elizabeth. "As long as we all have fun."

Cleo pushed T-Bone forward.

“Come on, T,” she said. “Let’s get ready!”

People started throwing snowballs.

T-Bone started running.

“Ahhh! Snowballs!” he shouted as he ran faster and faster.

T-Bone kept running.

He saw the other team's flag.

Hey, that flag can protect me from the snowballs, he thought.

T-Bone grabbed the flag.

He wrapped it around himself.

Then he ran quickly back to his team.

T-Bone hid behind his team's fort.

He was out of breath.

"You did it, T-Bone!" shouted Clifford.

"You have no snow on you, T!" shouted Cleo.

Clifford lifted T-Bone onto his back.

Everyone clapped and cheered.

"Hooray for T-Bone!" everyone yelled.

"Hooray for T-Bone," Jetta said quietly.

“So, what would you like for your prize,

T-Bone?” Clifford asked.

“Well, I got the best prize of all,” said T-Bone.

“I’m not afraid anymore.

That snowball fight was a lot of fun!”

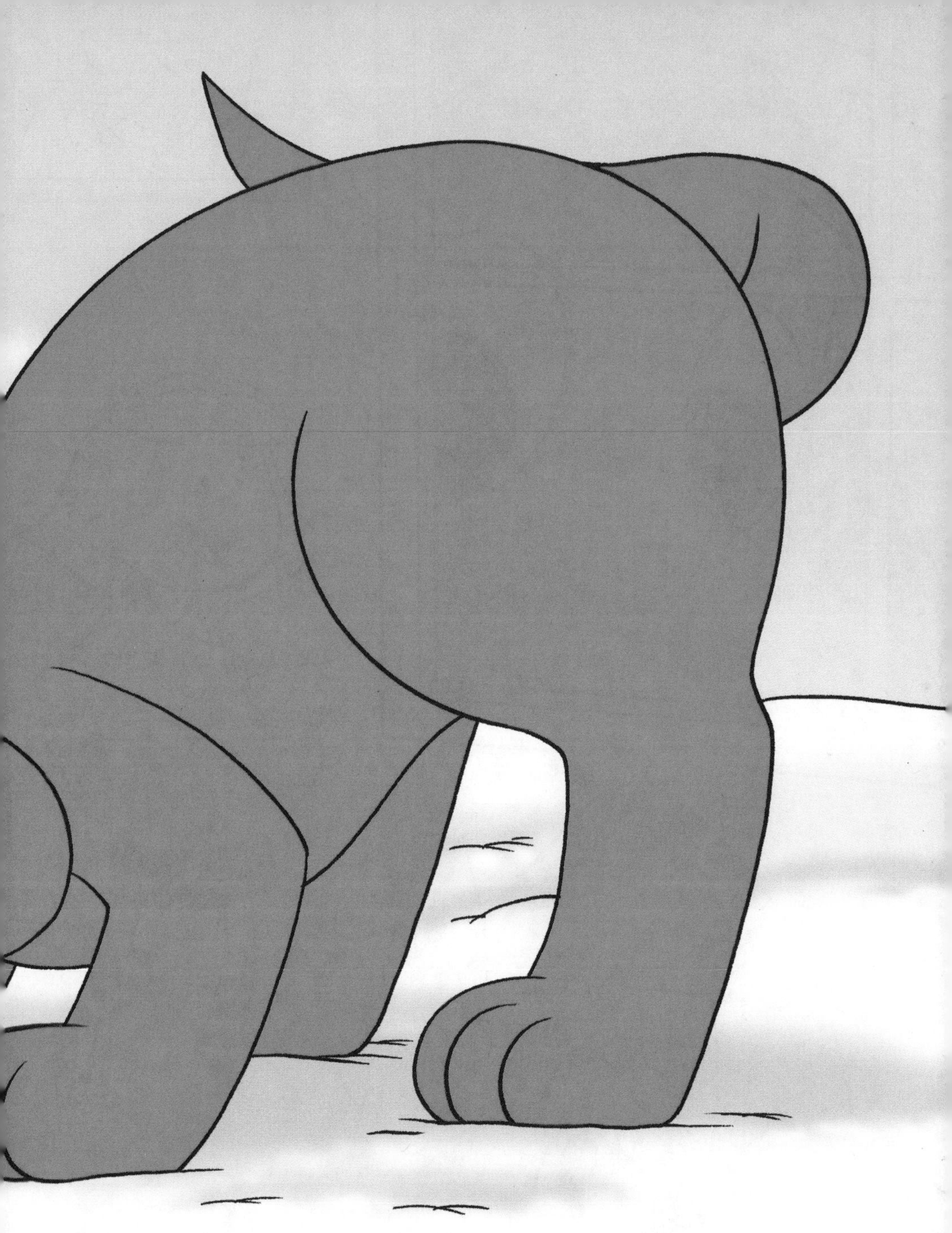

“I do have an idea, though,” said T-Bone.

“Why don’t we all go to a warm house and have some snacks?”

Everyone agreed that T-Bone's idea was great.

Especially T-Bone.

Do You Remember?

Circle the right answer.

1. Why doesn't T-Bone like snowball fights?
   - a. The snow is too cold.
   - b. He doesn't like getting hit with snowballs.
   - c. He'd rather eat snow cones.

2. Why does T-Bone grab the other team's flag?
   - a. To protect himself from the snowballs
   - b. Because the flag makes a nice outfit
   - c. Because he knows that's how to win the game

Which happened first?

Which happened next?

Which happened last?

Write a 1, 2, or 3 in the space after each sentence.

The teams built forts. 1

Everyone enjoyed some snacks. 3

T-Bone became the snowball fight champion. 2

Answers:

1. b
2. a

The teams built forts. (1)
Everyone enjoyed some snacks. (3)
T-Bone became the snowball fight champion. (2)